P9-CEY-413

Give Me Back My Pony

Do you love ponies? Be a Pony Pal!

Look for these Pony Pal books:

Pony Pal #1 I Want a Pony

Pony Pal #2 A Pony for Keeps

Pony Pal #3 A Pony in Trouble

coming soon

Pony Pal #5 Pony to the Rescue

PONY PALS®

Give Me Back My Pony

Jeanne Betancourt

illustrated by Paul Bachem

A
LITTLE APPLE
PAPERBACK

SCHOLASTIC INC.
New York Toronto London Auckland Sydney

If you purchased this book without a cover, you should be aware that this book is stolen property. It was reported as "unsold and destroyed" to the publisher, and neither the author nor the publisher has received any payment for this "stripped book."

No part of this publication may be reproduced in whole or in part, or stored in a retrieval system, or transmitted in any form or by any means, electronic, mechanical, photocopying, recording, or otherwise, without written permission of the publisher. For information regarding permission, write to Scholastic, Inc., 555 Broadway, New York, NY 10012.

ISBN 0-590-48586-5

Text copyright © 1995 by Jeanne Betancourt.
Illustrations copyright © 1995 by Scholastic Inc.
All rights reserved. Published by Scholastic Inc.
APPLE PAPERBACKS is a registered trademark of Scholastic Inc.

12   9/9 0/0

Printed in the U.S.A.   40

First Scholastic printing, May 1995

For my nephew, Chase

The author thanks her riding teachers, Linda Bushnell of Fair Weather Farm and Jeannette van Mill of Moles Hill Farm.

Thanks also to Elvia Gignoux and Helen Perelman for editorial assistance.

Contents

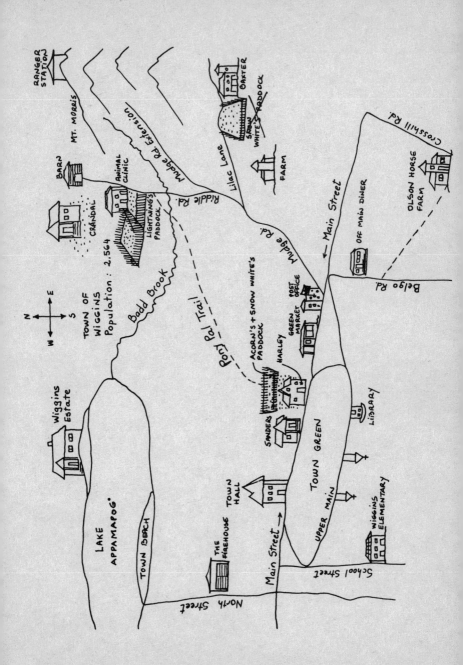

Give Me Back My Pony

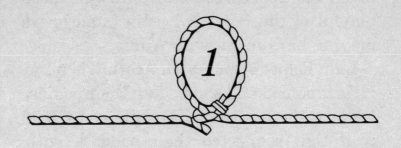

The Last Trail Ride

Lulu Sanders snapped her saddlebag closed and hurried out the back door. It was the first day of summer vacation and the Pony Pals were meeting on Pony Pal Trail for a whole day with their ponies.

By the time Lulu climbed the paddock fence, her pony, Snow White, was there to greet her. "I love you, Snow White," Lulu said, giving the white pony a hug.

Anna Harley, who lived next door, was climbing over the fence, too. But her pony didn't run up to her. Instead, Acorn scooted in the opposite direction. He was the most playful of the Pony Pal ponies and loved playing hard-to-get with Anna.

Lulu helped Anna catch Acorn. Then the girls groomed and saddled up their ponies. Finally, they rode onto the mile-and-a-half trail that connected their paddock with Pam Crandal's paddock.

Pam and Lightning met them halfway up Pony Pal Trail. "It's hot enough to take the ponies into the lake," Pam said.

"Great!" said Anna. "It'll be the first time this summer. I just know they'll love being in the water." The girls directed their ponies onto the Wiggins estate. The trails there led to Lake Appamapog.

When they reached the lakefront, Snow White pawed playfully at the wet sand. Lulu directed Snow White with her seat and her legs to go forward into the water. Snow White neighed as she walked into the cool lake. Anna followed on Acorn. Lightning was more timid than the other ponies about going into the lake. But when she saw Acorn and Snow White happily prancing around in the shallow water, she went in, too. The girls laughed and hooted as the water splashed up around their ponies' legs.

After playing in the lake, the ponies took naps under the trees while the Pony Pals ate their lunch. The girls agreed that the lake was a great new place to have fun with their ponies.

"Let's take them here again tomorrow," Pam said.

"I heard on the radio that tomorrow's going to be even hotter than today," Lulu said.

"We'll do it all sum — " Anna stopped in the middle of the word. The Pony Pals exchanged sad glances. They were remembering that soon Lulu wouldn't have a pony. Any day now, Snow White's *real* owner, Rema Baxter, would be coming home from boarding school. Then Lulu would have to give Snow White back. They also remembered that Lulu was going to move away very soon.

"I just can't believe you won't be here anymore, Lulu," Anna said. "Nothing will be the same without you."

"Lulu, do you know where you and your dad are going to live yet?" Pam asked.

"Not yet," Lulu answered. "It'll probably be someplace far away though. Like Africa. He mostly likes to write about large animals, like elephants."

Lulu had been living with her grandmother while her father worked on a wildlife research project in the Amazon jungle in Brazil. Lulu's mother died when Lulu was four years old. She wasn't so sad about not having a mother because she was very close to her father. She was glad that she and her dad would be together again soon. But that would mean leaving Wiggins and her Pony Pals.

"Wherever you go," Pam said, "I sure hope they have ponies."

"No pony can ever take the place of Snow White," Lulu said.

After lunch the girls put the bridles back on their ponies, mounted, and rode back to the trail. "Come on, don't be sad," Lulu said to her friends. "Let's have as much fun as we can while I'm still here." Then she moved Snow White into a canter.

Anna and Acorn started to canter, too. "Let's trail ride every day," Anna shouted.

Pam and Lightning cantered up beside Anna and Acorn. "And have barn sleep-overs," Pam added.

When the Pony Pals came off Pony Pal Trail at Pam's house, Lulu saw the five-year-old Crandal twins, Jack and Jill, running toward them.

"Lulu, your grandma called. Rema's father called her to ask where was Snow White," shouted Jill.

"You gotta bring Snow White back right now," shouted Jack.

Mrs. Crandal came up beside Lulu and Snow White and explained everything very

5

clearly. Rema Baxter was coming home from boarding school the next day. The Baxters had already put in a new paddock fence and ordered feed and straw. They wanted Snow White settled in her own field and stable, for Rema.

"Mr. Baxter seemed annoyed that he couldn't reach you all day," Mrs. Crandal added. "So you'd better take Snow White right over."

Lulu pressed her cheek against Snow White's warm, smooth neck as she listened to Mrs. Crandal. She thought about the wonderful time she and Snow White had that morning playing in the lake and trail riding. Today was their last trail ride and she hadn't even known it.

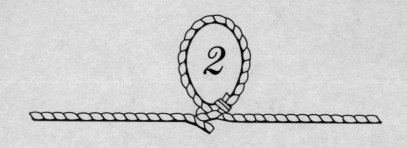

Getting Ready for Rema

"Oh, Lulu, I wish you didn't have to give Snow White back," Anna said.

"We'll go to the Baxters' with you," Pam told her.

The Pony Pals got on their ponies and rode them down Riddle Road toward the Baxters' property.

Turning left onto Lilac Lane, Lulu remembered when she saw the beautiful white pony caught in an old barbed wire. Everyone said that Lulu had saved Snow White's life. But she couldn't have done it without Pam and Anna. That was how they all had met — rescuing Snow White. Lulu always thought of that day as the beginning of the Pony Pals.

Lulu would miss her friends terribly when she left Wiggins. Anna Harley lived right next door to Lulu's grandmother. Their ponies shared the paddock behind the Harleys' house. Lulu thought Anna was a great friend. She was funny and full of energy. She was also a terrific artist.

Lulu trotted Snow White up beside Anna and Acorn. "When we're pen pals," she told Anna, "don't worry about spelling mistakes, okay? Just be sure to write. And draw me pictures, too." Anna promised she would.

Lulu knew there wouldn't be any spelling errors in Pam's letters. Pam Crandal got A's in all her subjects at school. But Lulu was afraid that Pam would be too busy to write her letters. The Crandals ran an animal clinic on their property. Dr. Crandal was a veterinarian, and Mrs. Crandal taught horseback riding. There were always a lot of animals at the Crandals', which meant a lot of chores for Pam.

Pam, bringing up the rear, called out, "Don't worry, Lulu. I'll find time to write you. I'll write every week." Lulu sometimes thought that the Pony Pals could read one another's minds.

When they reached the Baxters' property, the three girls dismounted. The new fence looked safe for ponies. But the girls made sure that there weren't any pieces of barbed wired left in the field. They knew how dangerous barbed wire could be from having seen what it did to Snow White. After they let their ponies into the paddock, they went to the stable to make sure it was ready for Snow White, too.

"This stable is filthy!" Pam shouted when they walked through the stable door.

Lulu could see that Pam was right. There were piles of dirty straw, dust, and cobwebs everywhere. The supplies had been delivered, but no one had put them away. "I can't

leave Snow White in this mess," Lulu said. "What if she gets into that food and over-eats? What if she wants to lie down in her stall?"

"Let's get to work," Pam said.

Anna started sweeping, Pam unloaded feed into the bins, and Lulu cleaned out the water buckets. Lulu felt a little nudge on her back. She turned around to see that Snow White had come up to her. The pony looked at Lulu as if to say, "What's going on? When are we going home?"

"This is your real home," Lulu told Snow White. "I was just taking care of you while Rema was away at school. You'll remember her when you see her tomorrow."

Snow White snorted and went back to Acorn and Lightning.

"I don't think Snow White even recognizes this place," Lulu told Anna and Pam.

"She only lived here a few weeks before you got her," said Pam. "The Baxters are new to Wiggins."

"That means Rema won't know any kids when she's home this summer," Lulu said. "Maybe she could go trail riding with you guys."

"Rema! A Pony Pal?" Anna exclaimed. "Never! I can't stand her. She's so snobby."

Pam and Lulu couldn't help laughing. "You've never even met her, Anna," Pam pointed out.

Lulu put a hand on Anna's shoulder. "You've got to give Rema a chance," she said. "For Snow White's sake. Snow White's going to really miss Acorn and Lightning."

"Well, I'll let Rema ride with us only because of Snow White," Anna said. "But she'll never be a Pony Pal."

"She's too old anyway," Pam said to Anna. "She's around fourteen. Like your sister. Maybe we should introduce them."

"If *I* don't like Rema," Anna responded, "my sister won't either."

Lulu hoped with all her heart that Anna

was wrong about Rema Baxter. She wanted Rema to be the nicest person in the world. For Snow White's sake.

The three girls made a final inspection of the stable.

"Couldn't be cleaner," Pam said.

"We've done everything," said Anna.

"There's one thing I haven't done," Lulu told the others.

"What?" Anna and Pam asked in unison.

"I haven't said good-bye to Snow White."

"You want us to wait for you?" Pam asked.

"I think I want to be alone with Snow White," Lulu said.

As Pam and Anna rode off on their ponies, Snow White neighed and ran along the fence. She seemed to be saying, "Where are you going without me? Hey, wait up."

Lulu played with Snow White for a while. First they chased one another around the paddock. Then they stood under the shade of a tree and Lulu sang Snow White some of the pony's favorite songs, like "Jingle Bells." Finally, Lulu gave Snow White a bucket of water and a handful of oats. She wrote a note and posted it on the stable door.

Dear Mr. and Mrs. Baxter:
   Snow White has eaten her dinner.
      Sincerely,
      Lucinda (Lulu) Sanders

P.S.
Tell Rema I said "Welcome, home."
P.P.S.
Snow White is the most wonderful
pony in the world.

Lulu rubbed Snow White's smooth white neck and told the pony, "Rema will be home tomorrow." She gave Snow White a hug and a kiss. Snow White sighed. "I'll never forget you, Snow White," Lulu said.

Lulu didn't want Snow White to see her cry. So she didn't look back when she climbed over the fence and ran down Lilac Lane. She was still running — and sobbing — when she turned the corner onto Mudge Road.

"Lulu! Wait!" Lulu looked up to see Pam and Anna walking toward her — without their ponies.

"We came to walk you home," Anna said.

The three friends held hands as they walked toward Main Street. No one spoke. Lulu knew that Pam and Anna felt sad about Snow White. They were her best friends. Soon she would be saying good-bye to them, too.

"I hate saying good-bye," Lulu said sadly.

"Me too," Pam said.

"Me three," Anna said.

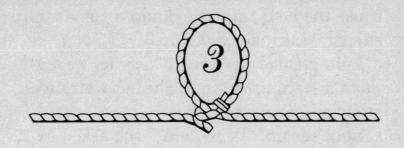

The Runaway Pony

When Lulu arrived home, she was still feeling sad. But her grandmother greeted her with some news that cheered her up. They had gotten a telegram from Lulu's father.

Leaving Jungle.
In U.S.A. Tuesday.
Love. Dad.

Lulu was so happy and excited about seeing her dad, she had a hard time falling asleep that night. But she must have, because the next thing she knew a voice was saying, "Lucinda, wake up."

Lulu opened her eyes to see her grandmother leaning over her. She had a strange smile on her face.

Lulu sat up. "Is he here?" she asked excitedly. "Is Dad here?"

"Not yet," her grandmother said. "It's only Sunday. But someone else is here."

"Who?" Lulu asked.

"That pony of yours," Grandmother answered.

"Snow White?!" Lulu shouted. "But I gave her back to Rema."

Lulu jumped out of bed and ran to the window. Grandmother was right. Snow White was in the paddock nibbling dewy grass next to Acorn. Just like always.

Lulu ran down the stairs and outside.

Anna was running across the yard, too. "I just saw Snow White out the kitchen window," she said to Lulu excitedly. "I was going to get you."

The two girls went into the paddock. Snow White neighed and ran over to them. "Snow White," Lulu said, "you ran away."

"She didn't run away," Anna said. "To her *this* is home. She ran home to Acorn and to you." Anna stroked the pony's neck. "What a smart pony."

"I better go back in and call the Baxters," Lulu said.

But the Baxters weren't home. Mr. Baxter's voice on the answering machine asked callers to leave a message. Lulu told the machine, "Snow White came back to the paddock she lived in when I was taking care of her. She didn't get hurt or anything. I'm bringing her back to you. Oh . . . this is Lulu Sanders. Thank you. Bye."

By the time Lulu had breakfast and went back outside, Pam and Lightning were also in the paddock.

"I bet the Baxters didn't even notice that Snow White was missing," Pam said. "They shouldn't have a pony."

"It's not their pony," Lulu said. "It's Rema's. Let's bring Snow White back."

"I bet she'll just run away again," Anna said.

"That'd be awful," Pam said. "It's dangerous for a pony to be loose on the roads. She could get hit by a truck or something."

"I know," Lulu said. "But she won't run away when Rema's there."

Lulu thought about Rema and Snow White. She hadn't pictured them together before. There would be another girl giving Snow White good-morning hugs. Another girl riding her and cantering like the wind. Another girl singing Snow White songs and grooming her.

"We better go," Lulu told her friends.

Lulu borrowed a bridle from Anna. Then, because she didn't have a saddle anymore, Lulu mounted Snow White bareback. "Let's take Pony Pal Trail instead of Main Street," she said. "It'll be safer."

The Pony Pals never thought they would

trail ride together again, and here they were on Pony Pal Trail.

"I missed us all riding together like this," Anna said.

"We just did it yesterday," Pam said.

"I know," said Anna. "But I miss it already."

When they got to the Baxters' and saw that Rema wasn't home yet, Pam said, "We'll wait here with you. We can help you explain how Snow White ran away and everything."

While they all waited for Rema, Lulu groomed Snow White one more time. She wanted Snow White to look her best. She was combing out Snow White's mane when the Baxters' station wagon pulled into the driveway. The instant the car stopped, a girl jumped out of the back and ran toward the paddock. "Snow White!" she called out. "Snow White, I'm home."

Snow White pulled away from Lulu, neighed happily, and cantered toward the girl. Rema was back.

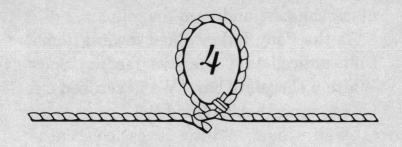

Meeting Rema

Lulu was standing in the middle of the paddock watching the happy reunion between Rema and Snow White.

Pam put her hand on Lulu's shoulder. "Come on, Lulu, let's tell Rema how Snow White ran away."

The Pony Pals walked toward Rema. "I don't like her," Anna whispered. "She's definitely a snob."

Lulu thought Rema looked nice. You could tell right away that she was older than the Pony Pals. She was taller than they were, had on a black sundress and black sandals, and used makeup.

As the Pony Pals walked toward Rema, they noticed that she was feeding Snow White a chocolate bar. "We never feed our ponies candy," Anna said.

"Well, Snow White loves chocolate," Rema said. "Who are you, anyway?"

"I'm Lulu Sanders," Lulu said. "We were waiting for you and keeping Snow White company."

"I'm Pam Crandal," Pam said. She extended her hand to shake with Rema's. Lulu wished she had thought of shaking hands, too.

"I'm Anna Harley," Anna said grumpily. Rema put out her hand to shake with Anna, but Anna pretended that she didn't see it.

"Snow White missed Lulu so much that she escaped and came back to our paddock," Anna said. "That's where she's been living with my pony, Acorn. Snow White missed Acorn, too. Our ponies are all best friends."

Rema stared at Lulu.

Lulu stared right back at her.

No one said a word.

Finally, Rema broke the silence. "So you're Lucinda Sanders," she said. "If I'd known you were so young I wouldn't have left my horse with you. You sounded older in your letters."

"Lulu knows all about *horses,*" Pam said. "And *ponies* like Snow White. She took very good care of your *pony.*"

"Is that why my *horse* ran away last night?" Rema asked.

Lulu felt awful. Why was Rema being mean to them? And why did she insist on calling Snow White a horse? Rema must know that Snow White was a pony breed and too small to be a horse. Was that what Anna would call "snobby"? It also bothered Lulu that Snow White was staying right next to Rema. She knew it was important that Snow White like her owner. But she hated that Snow White was ignoring her.

"Let's get out of here," Pam told Anna and Lulu. "I'll get Lightning."

While Pam and Anna went to get their ponies, Lulu told Rema, "We fixed up the stable for Snow White. She's been having two handfuls of oats everyday. One at —"

"I know how to take care of Snow White," Rema said. She ruffled up the hair on Snow White's forehead. "We've been together for a long time."

Snow White noticed that Lightning and Acorn were being saddled up. She walked over to Lulu and looked at her as if to say, "Okay, let's go."

"You're not going with us, Snow White," Lulu told the pony. But Snow White didn't understand. She neighed and gently nudged Lulu. To Lulu she was saying, "Come on. I want to go trail riding too."

"I'm sorry, Snow White," she whispered. "I wish you could come with us." Lulu combed out the hair on the pony's forehead that Rema had messed up.

Rema, meanwhile, was picking Snow White's white hair off her sundress. She didn't even look up when she asked Lulu,

"What do people around here do all summer? Wiggins is so boring."

"That's what I thought when I first moved here," Lulu said. "But it's really not boring at all. We go trail riding and swim in the lake. There're a lot of hiking trails. And there's a diner with really good food. Especially brownies. Sometimes we hang out there."

"I wasn't asking what *you* do," Rema said. "I meant the teenagers. Like me."

Lulu was beginning to think Anna was right about Rema Baxter. She hoped that Rema was nicer to ponies than she was to kids.

Snow White was still confused about why she wasn't being saddled up like Lightning and Acorn. The pony went over to Rema to see if she would tell her. A little string of Snow White's saliva fell on Rema's dress. "Oh, Snow White," Rema said with exasperation. "Now look what you've done!" She pushed Snow White away from her.

The Pony Pals exchanged glances. Rema

treated ponies the same way she treated people. None of them wanted to leave Snow White with this girl.

They knew they would have to come up with some good Pony Pal ideas of how to save Snow White from Rema. They also knew that they didn't have time to have a private meeting. Something had to be done now.

Pam stepped forward. "Rema," she said, "Snow White might try to run away again. That could be dangerous because of cars and everything."

Anna added her idea. "Maybe Snow White should stay in the paddock with Acorn at night. That way you'll know she's safe."

Now it was Lulu's turn. "I could pick Snow White up here around six at night and bring her back first thing in the morning. I could take care of her for you, too. I'd even do stuff like wash out her water bucket and clean up the paddock."

"And when Lulu moves away, Anna and I could do all those things," Pam added.

Rema laughed right in their faces. "I can take care of my own horse, thank you very much," she said. "I might as well. There isn't anything else to do around here. And don't worry about Snow White. She won't be getting out at night anymore. I'm going to keep her in the stable most of the time."

Lulu's heart sank. She knew that Snow White was just like her. They both wanted to be outside as much as possible. Now Snow White was going to be locked up in a stable. Poor Snow White.

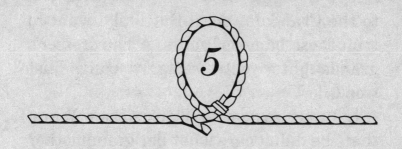

The Surprise

That night the Pony Pals were having their last barn sleepover.

As Lulu ate dinner with her grandmother, she was remembering all the great sleepovers she'd had with her friends. The girls would sleep in the barn while their ponies stayed out all night in the paddock. But tonight, while Acorn and Lightning were in the big Crandal paddock, Snow White would be alone in a cramped, hot stable.

Her grandmother interrupted Lulu's unhappy thoughts by saying, "I'll drive you to the Crandals', dear. But first I want to trim those bangs of yours. A hairdresser's grandaughter with straggly bangs just won't do."

Lulu was so depressed about Snow White that she didn't care what her grandmother did to her hair. She even let her give her a few curls.

"I'll miss you," Grandmother said as she fancied up Lulu's hair. "It's been wonderful having my granddaughter here. I'll even miss looking out the window and seeing that pretty pony of yours."

"Snow White's not my pony, Grandma," Lulu said sadly. "She's Rema Baxter's pony."

When Lulu got to Pam's house, she went directly to the paddocks and barn. But Anna and Pam weren't there. They must be in the kitchen, Lulu thought. She ran across the yard toward the house.

But there was no one in the kitchen except Woolie, the Crandals' dog.

"Anybody home?" Lulu called out.

"In here," Pam called back. "In the living room."

As Lulu and Woolie walked down the short hall to the living room, Lulu noticed that the house was strangely quiet. She pushed the living room door open. But no one was there.

"Pam?" Lulu said nervously. "Where are you?"

Suddenly people were coming at Lulu from *everywhere*.

The twins jumped out of their big toy box.

Dr. and Mrs. Crandal stepped out of a closet.

Anna's entire family rose up from behind the couch.

Grandmother Sanders, Pam, and the Pony Pals' friend, Ms. Wiggins, popped out from behind the drapes.

"SURPRISE!"

Everyone was yelling and laughing. Woolie was barking and jumping around.

Lulu was speechless. A surprise party just for her! It was the most wonderful surprise she'd ever had.

The dining room was decorated with periwinkle-blue streamers and balloons. "All the decorations are the Pony Pal color," Anna said, beaming.

"It's perfect," Lulu said.

In the middle of the table there was a huge brownie baked in the shape of a horseshoe. "For good luck," Anna's mother told Lulu.

Jill stood on a chair to put a wreath of daisies on Lulu's head. Jack had made a wreath, too. His was made of straw. "Because you love horses so much," he told her as he placed his wreath on top of Jill's.

And there were other presents. Ms. Wiggins gave Lulu a blank book with a red-plaid cloth cover. "It's for keeping a journal," she told Lulu. "You and your father live in such interesting places you really should keep a journal." Pam and her parents gave her a book called *The Ultimate Horse Book,* by Elwyn Hartley Edwards. Grandmother gave Lulu a fancy hairbrush-and-comb set. And Anna gave her a portrait she'd painted of Snow White!

Later, after the party was over, the Pony Pals went out to the paddock to say good night to Acorn and Lightning. Then they went into the barn and crawled into their sleeping bags.

"Thank you for the party," Lulu said. "It was the best."

"We thought of inviting Rema," Pam said.

"And then we met her," Anna added.

"Poor Snow White," they said in unison.

They were all silent for a few seconds, thinking about how Snow White was missing their last sleepover.

"I liked living in Wiggins," Lulu said. "Maybe Rema will like it, too. Maybe then she'll be a nicer person."

"I doubt it," Anna grumbled.

"I wonder where you'll live next, Lulu," Pam said.

"Wherever it is," Anna added, "I hope you'll like it as much as Wiggins."

"No place can be as good as Wiggins," Lulu said. "Because no place else will have the Pony Pals."

"I know what you mean," said Anna. "How could it?"

Pam and Lulu laughed.

"Did that sound conceited?" Anna asked.

"No," Lulu answered. "It sounded true. No one can replace you guys."

They fell asleep talking about all the Pony Pal adventures they'd had together.

Lulu dreamt about Snow White. In the dream she heard the pony crash against the side of a stall. The noise was so loud that the crash woke her up. But the noise wasn't a dream. It was *real*. Lulu knew there weren't any horses in the barn that night. But someone — or *something* — was in the barn. Anna reached over and grabbed Lulu's arm. The noise woke her up, too. Without saying a word, they woke up Pam. All three of them heard a loud grunt.

Lulu grabbed her flashlight. Without making a sound, the three girls wiggled out of their sleeping bags. The Pony Pals were going to find out whoever — or whatever — was in the barn.

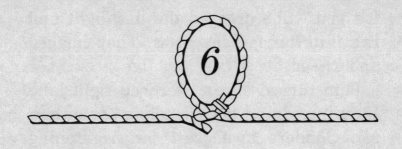

Bears!

What horrible, grunting creature was in the barn? The Pony Pals tiptoed out of the stall into the corridor. The barn was so dark they couldn't even see one another. Then Lulu pointed her flashlight into the blackness and turned the light on. In the beam of yellow light the Pony Pals saw the back of a huge . . . man.

They screamed.

The man screamed, too. He turned around to face them.

"HELP!" Pam and Anna yelled.

"Dad!" Lulu yelled. "Oh, Daddy, it's you. It's you." She dropped the flashlight and ran into her father's arms. They hugged and kissed.

Pam turned on an overhead light, and Lulu introduced her friends to her father. Mr. Sanders apologized for frightening them and explained that in the dark he had tripped over a wooden stool. "I forgot to bring a flashlight," he explained.

"You made such a weird noise when you fell," Pam said.

"Like this?" Mr. Sanders asked. He grunted again. The girls laughed. "Hey," Mr. Sanders said, "it's about time for the sun to rise. Let's watch together."

Pam said the hayloft was the best place to watch the sunrise. The Pony Pals and Mr. Sanders sat on bales of hay and faced the east through the hayloft window.

"Dad, I thought you weren't coming home until Tuesday," Lulu said.

"I made better plane connections than I expected," he told her. "When I got to your grandmother's, she told me you were here. I came right over. I figured I'd surprise you."

"You sure did!" the Pony Pals said in unison.

Lulu's father put his arm around her and pulled her close. "I just couldn't wait to see you."

"Me either," Lulu said. "I have so much to tell you."

The girls told Lulu's father about the surprise party. Then they talked about their ponies, especially Snow White. "I wish I still had Snow White so I could introduce you," Lulu said. "You just missed her." Then Lulu told her dad about giving Snow White back to Rema.

When the bottom curve of the sun had cleared Mount Morris, Lulu looked over to her dad. He had a little smile on his face and was staring at her. "Why are you looking at me like that?" she asked.

"I'm amazed at you," he said. "You've grown up so much in these past months.

You seem so independent and . . . responsible."

"That's because of Snow White," Lulu said. "I learned a lot from taking care of her." She looked over at Anna and Pam. "And I learned a lot from being a Pony Pal."

"We have Pony Pal Power," Anna explained. "When we work together on a problem, we can usually find a solution."

"Even when grown-ups can't," Pam added.

Now that the sun was up, they all went out to the paddock to introduce Mr. Sanders to Acorn and Lightning. They even showed him where Pony Pal Trail began at the edge of the paddock.

When Lulu and her father got into the car to go back to Grandmother Sanders', Lulu leaned out the car window and told her friends, "Go for a trail ride today and have fun. Don't worry about me. I have to pack and stuff. I'll see you before I leave town."

As they were driving along, Lulu asked

her father, "Where are we going to live next, Dad?"

Her father smiled at her but didn't answer.

"Come on, Dad. Where?"

"Lulu," her father began. "I missed you like crazy when I was working in the Amazon. And I know that you missed me. But I also know how happy you've been here in Wiggins."

"Dad, you're not going to leave me here and go away without me again. Please, Dad," Lulu pleaded. "I missed you so much."

"Let me finish," he said. "I've figured out a project for around here. I wrote a proposal." He looked over at Lulu again. "And I found out yesterday I got a grant to do it. For now, we'll both be living in Wiggins!"

"What animal will you study, Dad?" Lulu asked. "I bet it's the whitetail deer."

"Nope," he said. "I'm doing a research project on the black bear. They've been coming back to this region."

"Bears!" Lulu exclaimed. She couldn't wait to tell Pam and Anna. "That's neat, Dad. Can I help you?"

"Sure," he said. "Just like always."

Lulu smiled at her dad as they pulled into the driveway. She loved living in Wiggins. She was happy that she could stay with Pam and Anna, and be with her dad. But Lulu's smile disappeared when she thought of Snow White.

"What's wrong, Lulu?" her father asked. "I thought you'd be glad."

"I am," Lulu said. "I really am." Lulu tried to smile again. But it was hard. How could she live in Wiggins without Snow White?

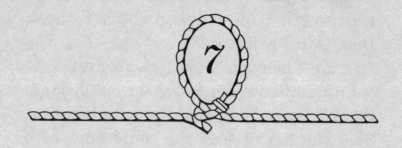

Not a Very Good Rider

After breakfast, Lulu's father went upstairs to take a nap. "He's exhausted from his long trip," her grandmother said. "He'll sleep all day."

The front doorbell rang. Grandmother's first client of the day had arrived. She'd be busy in her beauty parlor until dinnertime.

Lulu telephoned Pam's house. She wanted to tell Anna and Pam that she wasn't moving after all. Mrs. Crandal answered and told Lulu that the girls had already left for a day of trail riding on the Wiggins estate.

After Lulu did the breakfast dishes, she sat at the kitchen table. Now what would she do? If Snow White was still *her* pony, Lulu thought, she could go for a ride. Instead, Lulu sadly put on her hiking boots. She would go for a hike.

Lulu walked on Main Street until she reached Mudge Road. Then on Mudge Road she made a right onto Lilac Lane. Lulu was headed for the Baxters' paddock.

Lulu wasn't going to visit with Snow White. She knew that Snow White needed time to adjust to being with Rema again. But Lulu just had to check that Rema was letting Snow White out in the paddock during the day.

When she got close to the Baxter property, Lulu walked behind bushes on the other side of the road. She didn't want Snow White to see her. But there was no pony to hide from. Snow White wasn't in the paddock. Lulu checked carefully. No Snow White.

Was Rema keeping Snow White locked up in the stable all day long, too? How horrible! Lulu was feeling angry and trying to decide what to do next when she heard horses' hooves pounding on the dirt road.

She saw Rema trotting Snow White around a bend in Lilac Lane. But Rema's body wasn't in rhythm with Snow White's trot. Lulu wanted to call out, "Put your legs back!" She knew that if Rema corrected her seat, she and Snow White would both be more comfortable. Suddenly, Rema halted Snow White with a strong tug on the rein. The sides of Lulu's mouth ached in sympathy for the pony.

Rema leaned over the side of her saddle to adjust her stirrup. Then she moved Snow White back into a trot. But she still wasn't posting correctly. Lulu could see that Rema wasn't having a good time. And neither was Snow White.

"I don't know what's wrong with you,

Snow White," Rema said. "I shouldn't have let that kid take care of you. She ruined you for sure."

Lulu wanted to jump out from hiding to tell Rema, "That's not true. *You're* the one who doesn't know how to ride Snow White." But arguing with Rema wouldn't help anything. And shouting would only upset Snow White. Lulu decided to get out of there before she was discovered. She wanted to find her Pony Pals.

She turned to the dense woods behind her. There was a deer-run tunnel through the underbrush. She walked through it until the tunnel opened into a big square field where a dozen or so whitetail deer were grazing. Lulu moved silently around the edge of the field. One of the deer looked up and saw her. The deer let out a high-pitched warning shriek that sent the herd leaping into the woods.

By the time Lulu came to a road, she was hot and thirsty. But she didn't care. She needed to find the quickest way to the Wiggins estate. She needed to find Pam and Anna.

Lulu imagined her map of Wiggins. She was on Mudge Road Extension. Badd Brook ran parallel to Mudge Road. Following Badd Brook would be a perfect shortcut into the Wiggins estate.

Lulu had been walking along the brook for half an hour when she heard Acorn's familiar nicker. Just then Pam and Anna rode their ponies around a turn in the trail. Lulu noticed how sad her friends looked.

Pam was the first to see Lulu. Her sad look exploded into a big grin. "Look who's here," she told Anna.

"Lulu!" Anna screamed. "It's Lulu."

Lulu loved how happy her friends were to see her. They dismounted and led their ponies on foot so they could walk with Lulu. "Why did you guys look so miserable before?" Lulu asked. "What's wrong?"

"We were already missing you," Anna said.

"Well, forget that," Lulu told them. "Because I'm not moving after all. My dad's going to work on a project right here in Wiggins."

The Pony Pals yelled "Yes!" and hit high fives. Acorn and Lightning neighed, as if they understood the good news.

"And guess what else?" Lulu said.

"What?" Anna and Pam asked in unison.

"My dad's going to be studying black bears. They're coming back to this area. He's going to write an article about them for *National Geographic*."

"Bears!" Pam said.

"Great!" said Anna.

They did another round of high fives.

"And he said we could help him," Lulu added.

They did so many high fives that the palms of their hands stung.

"But I have some bad news, too," Lulu said. "Which is mainly why I came looking for you."

She told the other Pony Pals how she

spied on Rema and Snow White and that Rema was a terrible rider.

"I'm not surprised," Anna said.

"How did she win all those ribbons we saw hanging in the stable?" Lulu wondered out loud.

"Maybe she *was* a good rider," Pam said. "But she hasn't ridden in a long time. She must have forgotten a lot."

"She blames me for her bad riding," Lulu said. "I heard her tell Snow White."

"That's just like Rema to blame someone else for her problems," Anna said.

For once Pam and Lulu totally agreed with Anna's opinion of Rema.

"Lulu, you're the one who should be riding Snow White," Pam said.

"If you're going to be living in Wiggins, you should have her," Anna said.

"But how?" Lulu asked.

"We'll each come up with an idea of how you can get Snow White back," Pam said.

"Let's meet at the diner at seven o'clock

to put our ideas together," Anna suggested.

"Don't worry, Lulu," Pam said. "We'll come up with a Pony Pal plan for getting Snow White back."

"Remember, we have Pony Pal Power," Anna added.

The Pony Pals went to the field they liked best for jumping stone walls. Lulu took turns jumping Acorn and Lightning. But three girls with two ponies just wasn't the same as three girls with three ponies.

Lulu walked home along Pony Pal Trail beside her friends and their ponies. She missed Snow White so badly that tears came to her eyes. What if she couldn't get Snow White back?

Three Good Ideas

After dinner, Lulu asked her grandmother and father if she could go over to Off-Main Diner with her friends.

"What would you think of me coming along with you?" her father asked. "I'd like to meet some of my new neighbors."

"That'd be great," Lulu answered. "It's a very popular diner. Anna's mother owns it. We'll introduce you to lots of people."

Pam and Anna were waiting for Lulu on Anna's front porch. "My dad's coming, too," she explained. "But we can still have our meeting."

"What's the meeting about?" Mr. Sanders asked as they all headed down Main Street. "Or is it top secret?"

"We have to figure out how to get Snow White back for Lulu," Pam explained to Mr. Sanders.

"Lulu needs a pony," Anna added.

"My goodness," Mr. Sanders said, "of course she does. I've been so jet-lagged I haven't been thinking clearly. Wiggins is a great place to have a pony. Could Lulu still keep a pony in your paddock, Anna?"

"Sure," Anna answered.

"It's settled then," Mr. Sanders said. "We'll get you a pony, Lulu. That'll be terrific."

Anna and Pam cheered. And Lulu acted excited and thanked her dad. But she was thinking that the only pony for her was Snow White.

"I should introduce my father to some people before we have our meeting," Lulu whispered to Anna and Pam, "so he won't be alone."

"There's someone he should meet," Anna said as they walked into the diner. She was pointing to the counter where Ms. Wiggins was eating her dinner.

All the Pony Pals were friends with Ms. Wiggins. But Anna was closest to her because they were both dyslexic and they were both artists. Also, they both had Shetland ponies.

Ms. Wiggins looked up and saw the Pony Pals. "Hi, girls," she said. She looked right at Mr. Sanders and added, "I'll bet you're Lulu's father. You look so much alike."

"Why, thank you," Mr. Sanders said. He put an arm around Lulu's shoulder. "I consider that a huge compliment."

"As well you should," Ms. Wiggins said. She put out her hand.

Mr. Sanders smiled as he shook Ms. Wiggins' hand and said, "I'm Tom Sanders."

"I'm Winifred Wiggins. I'm glad to meet you, Tom. But I'm not glad you'll be taking Lulu away. We're all going to miss her."

"No, we're not," Anna said.

"We're not?" Ms. Wiggins asked with surprise.

"Nope," Anna said. "Because Lulu's not moving!"

They all laughed. Then Mr. Sanders told Ms. Wiggins that he was going to live in Wiggins for awhile.

"He's going to study black bears," Lulu explained. "And write an article about them."

Soon Ms. Wiggins and Mr. Sanders were sitting next to one another at the counter. She was telling him all about a black bear that she'd sighted on the Wiggins estate.

The Pony Pals made themselves ice-cream sodas and brought them to the back booth. It was time to go over their ideas for how to get Snow White back.

"It's great that your father said he'd buy you a pony, Lulu," Pam said.

"I'd rather *rent* Snow White than *buy* an-

other pony," Lulu said. "That's what my idea's about."

Lulu handed Pam a slip of paper. She read it aloud.

Lease Snow White from Rema.
Tell her she can still ride Snow
White whenever she wants.

"That way Rema can make some money and still ride," Lulu explained. "You can tell by the way she dresses that she likes to buy things. And, if she wants, I'll do all the stable chores."

"Rema must really hate mucking out," Anna commented.

"Lulu, I like your idea," Pam said. "If it works we should also try to get her to take some riding lessons. It sounds like she needs them."

"I'm not sure that she should be riding Snow White at all," Anna said. "That's what *my* idea is about." Anna put a drawing in the middle of the table.

Lulu and Pam laughed at the picture. "You got her perfect," Pam said. "You could draw cartoons for the newspaper."

"Rema's not *that* big," Lulu said.

"But I bet you anything she's too big for Snow White," Anna said. "She's taller than any of us. I bet that's why she has trouble riding."

"Why didn't I think of that?" Pam wondered out loud. "You're right, Anna. And it fits right in with *my* idea."

Pam gave her idea to Lulu to read out loud.

Get Rema to buy a horse so she'll sell Snow White to Lulu.

"Remember how she kept calling Snow White a horse instead of a pony?" Pam asked. "She thinks she's too grown-up for a pony. So she should get a horse. A big one. Then you can buy Snow White, Lulu."

"Olson's horse farm has tons of horses," Anna said. "Mr. Olson would have a good horse for Rema. Something like that black Morgan he tried to sell me would be perfect for her."

"We've got a lot to tell Rema," Lulu said. "But how are we going to get her to listen to us? She thinks we're just these little kids who don't know anything."

"Leave it to me," Pam said. "I'll call her up and *schedule* a *business meeting*. She loves that sort of thing."

"You're the best one to do it," Anna said to Pam.

Lulu agreed.

"What'll you say if she asks you what the meeting is about?" Anna asked.

"I'll tell her that it's too important to discuss on the phone," Pam answered.

"Rema will love that, too," said Anna.

Pam got up and went to the pay phone near the kitchen. In a few minutes she came back. "We're meeting at her place at ten o'clock tomorrow morning," Pam told them proudly.

The Pony Pals were glad. But they didn't hit high fives. They all knew that getting Rema Baxter to sell Snow White would be one of the toughest challenges the Pony Pals ever faced.

You Shrunk My Pony

The next morning the Pony Pals met on the town green. They were wearing their best clothes for the meeting with Rema Baxter.

As they walked along Lilac Lane toward the Baxters' property, they saw that Snow White wasn't in her paddock. "I told you, Rema locks her up during the day," Lulu said to the others.

By the time they rang the doorbell, the Pony Pals were more determined than ever to get Snow White back.

Rema let them in. "Good morning," she said. "Follow me." She led them down a hall and into the dining room.

Rema sat at the head of the table. She instructed Pam to sit to her right. Anna and Lulu were to sit on her left.

Before Pam could say why they were there, Rema said, "Lucinda Sanders, you have damaged my horse."

The Pony Pals were so surprised by what Rema said that for a second they were speechless.

Finally, Lulu said, "What are you talking about?"

"Lulu took the best care of Snow White," Pam said.

"She even saved her life!" Anna added.

"Is Snow White sick?" Lulu asked Rema in a hushed, frightened voice.

"If she's sick," Anna told Rema, "it's because you keep her locked up all the time."

"What are her symptoms?" Pam asked. "My father's a veterinarian. We can get him over here right away."

"My first complaint," Rema said, "is that you didn't feed her enough. She's lost weight so she's smaller than she used to be."

"Lulu fed Snow White plenty," Anna said. "Snow White didn't shrink."

"Don't interrupt," Rema scolded. "My second complaint is that Lucinda Sanders ruined Snow White's fine schooling. Snow White used to be an excellent ride. She doesn't work the same way since Lucinda rode her."

Pam stood up and spoke in a commanding voice. "Now it's our turn to talk, Rema Baxter. First of all, Snow White didn't lose weight. You are too tall for Snow White now, so she seems smaller to you."

"How much did you grow when you were away at school this year?" Anna asked.

"Two inches," Rema boasted.

"You were probably already too big for Snow White when you left for school. Now you're way too big," Pam told her.

"If you're not the right size for a pony,"

67

Lulu explained, "it doesn't feel right when you ride. It's uncomfortable for the pony, too."

"Why don't you sell Snow White and buy a horse that's the right size for you," Pam advised.

Rema tapped a pencil eraser on the table. She was deep in thought. The Pony Pals didn't say a word. They all had their fingers crossed under the table.

Finally, Rema broke the silence by wondering out loud, "But if I got a horse, what would I do with it when I went back to school?"

"Maybe you don't want a horse anymore," Pam suggested.

"I bet there's something else you'd like to do with the money you make by selling Snow White," Anna said. "Something you want very badly."

"There is," Rema exclaimed. "If I could make some quick money I could go to sleep-away camp this summer with my boarding school friends. Then I woudn't have to stay in boring Wiggins."

The Pony Pals smiled and nodded at Rema.

"Great idea," Anna said. "Sleep-away camp is so much fun." Anna winked at Lulu.

"I'd like to buy Snow White," Lulu told Rema.

"Okay," Rema said. "I'll sell you Snow White. But not for a penny less than . . . two thousand dollars."

The Pony Pals couldn't believe their ears. Lulu knew that her father wouldn't — couldn't — spend that much on a pony.

"You just made that number up," Anna said. "You don't know how much Snow White is worth."

"You need an expert to price a pony," Lulu said. "Like Mr. Olson."

"Mr. Olson buys and sells horses and ponies all the time," Pam explained to Rema. "He'd help you decide how much to charge for Snow White."

"All right," Rema said. "I'll talk to this Mr. Olson. I'll call him right now."

As Rema looked up Olson's phone number in the phone book, the Pony Pals exchanged little smiles. Mr. Olson would set a fair price. It still wasn't time for high fives, but at least there was a chance that Lulu could get Snow White back.

"Hello, Mr. Olson," Rema said into the phone. "I'm Rema Baxter and I have a prize pony to sell. She's a very special eight-year-old Welsh pony, thirteen-point-two hands high. She's very beautiful. I was wondering if you had any clients that might be interested."

Lulu waved her hand in front of Rema's face. "*I'm* interested. *I'm* the one who wants to buy Snow White."

Rema scowled at Lulu and continued her conversation with Mr. Olson.

When Rema hung up the phone, Lulu repeated, "I said I wanted to buy Snow White."

"I realize that, Lucinda," Rema said.

"But you're not the only one who might like to buy Snow White."

"But I took care of her," Lulu said.

"We're the ones who came up with the idea of selling her in the first place," Pam put in.

"You're not being fair," Anna complained.

"Lucinda, if you want to buy Snow White," Rema said, "come to Mr. Olson's farm at three o'clock. There'll be other people there who will be interested in buying her."

Rema led them to the door. "Thank you for coming by," she said. "I think we had a very productive meeting."

Sold!

Lulu's father was in the kitchen when Lulu got home. He looked rested and was eating a huge breakfast.

"Well, good morning," he said with a smile and wide-open arms.

Lulu gave her father a big hug. It was so wonderful to have him back. She sat on his knee and told him the news that Snow White was for sale.

"Perfect," her father said. "That's the pony we'll get. But I hope she's not a prize pony with fancy papers. We only have so much money we can spend for a pony."

Lulu wished she and Snow White hadn't won all those ribbons in the horse shows. She hoped that Snow White wasn't such a special pony, after all.

At two-thirty Lulu and her dad hiked over to Mr. Olson's. They were near the end of the shortcut trail between Off-Main Diner and the horse farm when Lulu heard the clippity-clop of horses behind them. Anna and Pam were riding their ponies over to Olson's to help Lulu buy Snow White.

When they came out at Olson's farm, Lulu saw Mr. Baxter's station wagon. There was another, very expensive car parked right next to the Baxters' car. Lulu guessed that anybody who had a car that fancy could afford an expensive prize pony.

"I know that car," Anna said.

"Whose is it?" Pam asked.

"Tommy Rand's mother's!" Anna answered.

The Pony Pals gasped. Tommy Rand was a mean, bossy kid in the eighth grade. He'd rented Acorn when he was in the fourth grade. The Pony Pals thought that Acorn must have had a terrible life with a kid like Tommy Rand. Did Tommy Rand want to buy Snow White?

"Tommy wouldn't want a pony," Pam said. "All he cares about is football and teasing girls."

"But his sister might," Anna said. "Look!"

They saw Mr. Olson leading Snow White around the side of the barn. With him were Tommy Rand, his sister Anita, Mrs. Rand, the Baxters, and Rema.

Pam and Anna dismounted their ponies and walked with Lulu and her father to the group gathered around Snow White.

"Hi, girls," Mr. Olson said cheerfully. "What can I do for you today?" He winked at Anna. "Ready to trade Acorn for my beautiful black Morgan?"

"You know I wouldn't give up Acorn," Anna told him.

"Well, look who's here. It's the Pony Pests," Tommy Rand said.

Anita ignored her brother and said a friendly hi to Pam, Anna, and Lulu. They knew Anita Rand from school and thought she was nice. They felt sorry for her because she had Tommy Rand for a brother.

Lulu gave Snow White a hello rub on the neck. She looked into the pony's eyes to tell her that she missed her and was trying to get her back. Snow White gently nudged Lulu's shoulder.

"I guess you girls came to say good-bye to Snow White." Mr. Olson patted Snow White on the shoulder. "She's a nice pony," he said. "A real winner."

"I'm here to *buy* Snow White," Lulu said.

"But I just bought her," Anita told Lulu.

"Anita rode her and liked her very much," Mrs. Rand explained. "And we've agreed to the price."

Lulu glared at Rema. "You said to come at three o'clock."

"Did I?" Rema said with a smile. "Well, I suppose you could bid on Snow White since you're here now. We could have a little auction."

"Why is anyone talking to these pests?" Tommy Rand asked. Lulu noticed that his mother just ignored him. So did the Pony Pals.

Mr. Olson was surprised by Rema's suggestion that they have a horse auction. "That's not how we work these things," Mr. Olson told her. "You asked me to suggest a price. I did. You accepted it. The Rands said they're willing to pay the amount."

Mrs. Baxter shot Rema an angry look. "Why didn't you tell me that the girl who saved Snow White's life wanted to buy her?" Mrs. Baxter asked Rema.

"Mom," Rema hissed. "We can make more money this way. It's good business."

"No, it's not," Mrs. Baxter said.

While Mrs. Baxter and Rema were talking, the Pony Pals were thinking. They needed three ideas — quick. This was their last chance to get Snow White back.

"I took care of Snow White while Rema was away at school," Lulu told Anita. "Snow White is a wonderful pony. I'm sure you'll love her. How long will you be trying her out?"

"Most people try a pony at least a week before the purchase is final," Pam said. "Isn't that right, Mr. Olson?"

"I insist on it," Mr. Olson said. "Unless they've leased the animal first. The Rands understand how it's done. A small deposit. A week's trial."

"And a veterinarian checkup to be sure Snow White is in perfect health," Pam added.

"Then," Mr. Olson continued, "we collect the rest of the money and the sale is final."

"Wait a minute," Rema said. "You mean I won't get all my money today?"

"That's how this business is done, young lady," her father said sternly.

Anna gave Acorn's reins to Pam and went over to the paddock where the black Morgan was grazing. "Look at this beautiful horse, Anita," she said. "Isn't he wonderful?"

"Oh, that Morgan is a beauty," Lulu said.

"I didn't see him before," Anita commented as she moved toward the paddock. The Morgan came over to the girls at the fence.

"I could see you on that Morgan, Anita," Pam said. "He's a little bigger than Snow White. But looking at your height and the Morgan's size, I'd say he's perfect for you."

Anita was hardly listening. She was looking deep into the eyes of the Morgan and rubbing his cheek.

"If you'd like, I could saddle him up so you could give him a try," Mr. Olson told Anita.

"Please," Anita said. "If it's not too late, I'd like to try him, too."

Mr. Baxter and Tommy Rand grumbled

and complained about the wait. Everyone else — except Rema — agreed that Anita should try the Morgan. When he was saddled up, Anita mounted and rode him around the ring a few times.

After her ride, Anita pulled him up alongside the paddock fence where everyone was waiting and watching. Mr. Olson told Anita, "Now that I've seen you ride both Snow White and the Morgan, I'd say the Morgan suits you better. What do you think?"

"I want the Morgan," Anita said. Then she cantered the horse around the ring again.

"Oh, great," Tommy Rand said. "Just great. We'll never get out of here."

"This isn't fair," Rema grumbled. "She already said she wanted Snow White."

Meanwhile, Lulu and her father exchanged a glance. Sometimes they understood one another without talking — just like the Pony Pals. "Mr. Baxter," said Mr.

Sanders, "I was wondering if you would tell me what price has been set for Snow White?"

Mr. Baxter whispered a figure in Mr. Sanders' ear. Lulu's father gave her the thumbs-up sign.

"Mr. Baxter," Lulu said, "if Anita would like to buy the Morgan, I would like to buy Snow White. I don't need a week to try her because I took care of her for a long time. We could finalize the sale right now."

"You mean I could get all the money today?" Rema said. "And go to camp?"

"The sooner the better," Anna mumbled.

"If the Sanders girl would like Snow White," Mrs. Rand said, "we would be happy to shift our deposit onto the Morgan."

Anita had dismounted. She laid her head on the Morgan's neck. "I already love him," she said. "And I don't even know his name. What is it?"

"Morgan," Mr. Olson and the Pony Pals answered in unison. Everyone laughed.

"What do you say, Mr. Baxter?" Mr. Olson asked.

"It's okay with me," Mr. Baxter said.

"Me too!" Rema exclaimed.

"So let's do some business here," Mr. Olson said. "Anita Rand takes Morgan on trial. And Lulu Sanders buys Snow White."

The Pony Pals shouted "Yes!" and hit high fives and danced around. Then Lulu gave Snow White a great big hug and kiss.

Snow White neighed, as if to say, "Can we go home now, Lulu?"

Dear Reader:

I am having a lot of fun researching and writing books about the Pony Pals. I've met many interesting kids and adults who love ponies. And I've visited some wonderful ponies at homes, farms, and riding schools.

Before writing Pony Pals I wrote fourteen novels for children and young adults. Four of these were honored by Children's Choice Awards.

I live in Sharon, Connecticut, with my husband, Lee, and our dog, Willie. Our daughter is all grown up and has her own apartment in New York City.

Besides writing novels I like to draw, paint, garden, and swim. I didn't have a pony when I was growing up, but I have always loved them and dreamt about riding. Now I take riding lessons on a horse named Saz.

I like reading and writing about ponies as much as I do riding. Which proves to me that you don't have to ride a pony to love them. And you certainly don't need a pony to be a Pony Pal.

Happy Reading,

Jeanne Betancourt

Pony Pals

Be a Pony Pal®!

❏ BBC0-590-48583-0	#1	I Want a Pony	$2.99
❏ BBC0-590-48584-9	#2	A Pony for Keeps	$2.99
❏ BBC0-590-48585-7	#3	A Pony in Trouble	$2.99
❏ BBC0-590-48586-5	#4	Give Me Back My Pony	$2.99
❏ BBC0-590-25244-5	#5	Pony to the Rescue	$2.99
❏ BBC0-590-25245-3	#6	Too Many Ponies	$2.99
❏ BBC0-590-54338-5	#7	Runaway Pony	$2.99
❏ BBC0-590-54339-3	#8	Good-bye Pony	$2.99
❏ BBC0-590-62974-3	#9	The Wild Pony	$2.99
❏ BBC0-590-62975-1	#10	Don't Hurt My Pony	$2.99
❏ BBC0-590-86597-8	#11	Circus Pony	$2.99
❏ BBC0-590-86598-6	#12	Keep Out, Pony!	$2.99
❏ BBC0-590-86600-1	#13	The Girl Who Hated Ponies	$2.99
❏ BBC0-590-86601-X	#14	Pony-Sitters	$3.50
❏ BBC0-590-86632-X	#15	The Blind Pony	$3.50
❏ BBC0-590-37459-1	#16	The Missing Pony Pal	$3.50
❏ BBC0-590-37460-5	#17	Detective Pony	$3.50
❏ BBC0-590-51295-1	#18	The Saddest Pony	$3.50
❏ BBC0-590-63397-X	#19	Moving Pony	$3.50
❏ BBC0-590-63401-1	#20	Stolen Ponies	$3.50
❏ BBC0-590-63405-4	#21	The Winning Pony	$3.50
❏ BBC0-590-74210-8		Pony Pals Super Special #1: The Baby Pony	$5.99
❏ BBC0-590-86631-1		Pony Pals Super Special #2: The Lives of our Ponies	$5.99
❏ BBC0-590-37461-3		Pony Pals Super Special #3: The Ghost Pony	$5.99

Available wherever you buy books, or use this order form.

....

Send orders to Scholastic Inc., P.O. Box 7500, Jefferson City, MO 65102

Please send me the books I have checked above. I am enclosing $_____ (please add $2.00 to cover shipping and handling). Send check or money order — no cash or C.O.D.s please.

Please allow four to six weeks for delivery. Offer good in the U.S.A. only. Sorry, mail orders are not available to residents of Canada. Prices subject to change.

Name_____ Birthdate ____/____/____

     First   Last   M   D   Y

Address_____

City_____ State_____ Zip_____

Telephone (_____)_____ ❏ Boy ❏ Girl

Where did you buy this book? ❏ Bookstore ❏ Book Fair ❏ Book Club ❏ Other